Nobody Rides
The Unicorn

Nobody Rides The Unicorn

~

Adrian Mitchell

Illustrated by
Stephen Lambert

PICTURE CORGI BOOKS

In the faraway land of Joppardy
there was once a King who was full of fear.
He was afraid of everybody in the world.
He was sure they were plotting to put poison
in his wine or in his food.

So the King called the most cunning man
in Joppardy, who was called Doctor Slythe.

"There is only one sure way to avoid being poisoned," said Doctor Slythe. "You must drink from a goblet made from a unicorn's horn. You must eat with a knife, fork and spoon made from a unicorn's horn."

"But how can I catch a unicorn?" asked the King. "Such a beast is too fierce and fast for my hounds."

Doctor Slythe whispered in his ear: "The unicorn can only be trapped by a quiet young girl with a gentle voice."

"So - find me that girl!" bellowed the King.

Doctor Slythe sent for Zoe, the beggar girl.
She was the quietest, gentlest girl in all Joppardy and nobody's child.

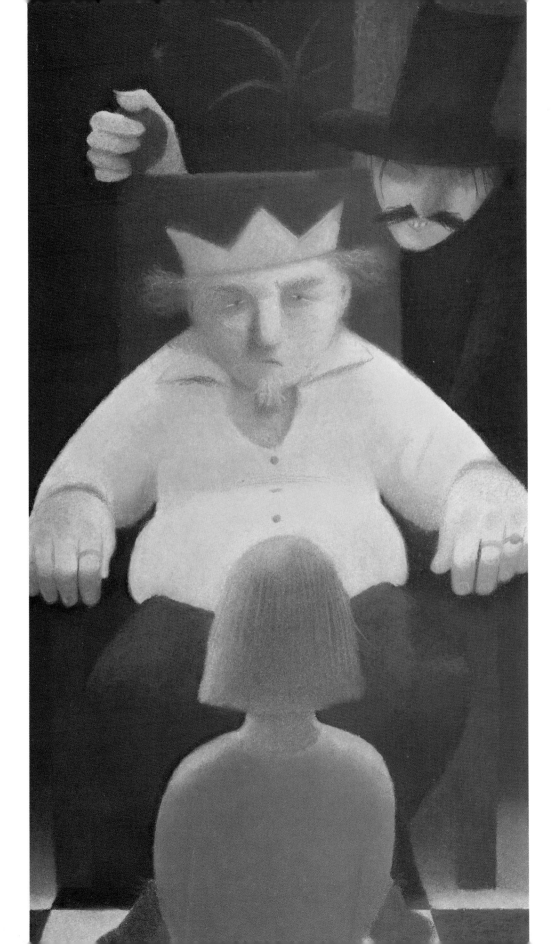

Zoe was brought before
the King. Doctor Slythe
told her:

"We will take you into the
deep forest
and you will sit alone
singing sweetly and softly.
After a while, perhaps, a
unicorn will appear
and come and lay his head
in your lap."

Zoe was very excited and scared, but she wanted to see the unicorn, So she went with the King and the Doctor into the deep forest and sat alone and waited under a silver birch tree and she sang, very sweetly and softly, this song, which she had learned to sing in her dreams:

"His coat is like snowflakes
Woven with silk.
When he goes galloping
He flows like milk.

His life is all gentle
And his heart is bold.
His single horn is magical
Barley sugar gold.

Nobody rides the Unicorn
As he grazes under a secret sun.
His understanding is so great
That he forgives us, every one.

Nobody rides the Unicorn,
His mind is peaceful as the grass.
He is the loveliest one of all
And he lives behind the waterfall."

Zoe looked down at the flowers round her feet while she sang, and when she looked up, there was the Unicorn.

His dark golden eyes gazed into her eyes. He snuffled and stamped his hooves on the earth. Then he lay down and put his head in her lap.

She said: "Good Unicorn, good Unicorn," and tickled him under the chin. His breathing was warm and musical and soon his dark golden eyes closed in sleep.

Suddenly the air was torn by trumpets. Out of the forest ran a hundred huntsmen. There was a terrible struggle and the Unicorn was wounded seven times by spears and hounds.

But he fought on until Doctor Slythe crept up behind him and threw a magical gold bridle round his neck.

And then the Unicorn stood still and allowed himself to be led out of the forest and down the road by the river and through the streets of the city and into the gardens of the Royal Palace.

And there the Unicorn was pushed into a paddock surrounded by a strong fence and the Unicorn was chained to a tree.

Now Zoe was very angry for she had been used to trick the Unicorn and now they had made it a prisoner and she knew that was wrong because unicorns can only live in freedom.

When she overheard the King and the Doctor planning to kill the Unicorn and make a goblet, and knives and forks and spoons out of its beautiful horn, Zoe was angry enough to burst.

But Zoe was clever, so she didn't burst. She hid her anger and, in the middle of the night, she crept into the gardens of the Royal Palace and cleaned the wounds of the Unicorn and set him free.

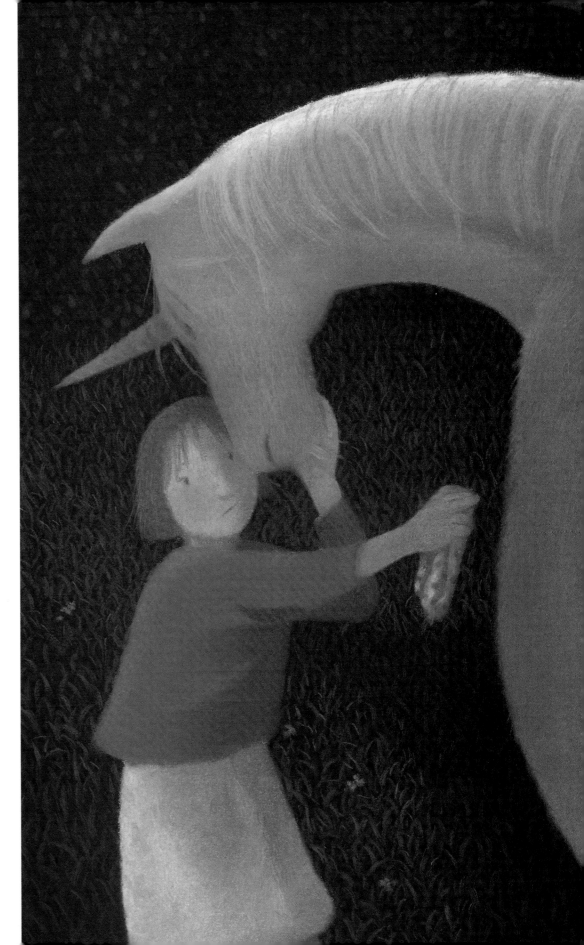

The Unicorn lowered his head once to her, and gazed into her eyes, then he neighed once and galloped off down the streets of the sleeping city along the road beside the river and into the depths of the forest.

When the King knew the Unicorn had escaped and Zoe had set him free, he shouted at her: "I ought to chop your head off! What do you say to that?" Zoe was the quietest girl in Joppardy, so she said nothing at all.

"You dare to be silent when I ask you a question?" screamed the King. "Very well, you shall have silence. I order that, from this day on, no-one in Joppardy shall speak to this little nobody!"

Zoe was in disgrace and she was
unhappy. She missed the Unicorn
terribly, but where could she find
him? Then she remembered those
lines from her dream song:
"He is the loveliest one of all
And he lives behind the waterfall."

Zoe left the city and followed the
road beside the river. A full moon
changed the river to silver. She
followed its shining as it wound its
way through the forest towards the
bright mountains.

Suddenly she was face to face with the waterfall. It was huge and powerful, like a giant of water. Zoe started to climb the waterfall. It was strong and icy and the cold hurt her hands so much that she cried as she climbed and the waterfall washed her tears away.

She missed her footing, and found herself falling in through the waterfall, and into a cave. There might have been snakes, there might have been bears – but Zoe only thought of the Unicorn as she scrambled through the cave towards a speck of light which became bigger and bigger till she came out at the other side.

She looked down into the Secret Valley of the Unicorns. There she saw the unicorns dancing together slowly in the moonlight.

Zoe sat down to watch them. She was so happy she began to sing. Her Unicorn turned away from the dancing and trotted over to Zoe.

His dark golden eyes gazed
into her eyes. He snuffled and
stamped his hooves on the
earth. Then he lay down and put
his head in her lap. She said:
"Good Unicorn, good Unicorn,"
and she tickled him under the
chin and she sang her dream
song, sweetly and softly.

At the end of Zoe's song, the
Unicorn's dark golden eyes spoke
to her, saying: "Tell me, my kind
friend, who are you?"
Zoe said: "Me, I'm nobody."

"Climb on my back, kind Nobody,"
said the Unicorn with his eyes.
"For Nobody rides the Unicorn."

So Zoe climbed on to his back and held on to his mane
and they trotted down into the Secret Valley of the Unicorns.

WIth love to Natasha, Charlotte, Caitlin,
Zoe, Arthur and Lola – my grandchildren   A.M.

For Flying Robert, wherever he may be   S.L.

NOBODY RIDES THE UNICORN
A PICTURE CORGI BOOK : 0 552 546178

First published in Great Britain by Doubleday,
a division of Transworld Publishers

PRINTING HISTORY
Doubleday edition published 1999
Picture Corgi edition published 2000

1 3 5 7 9 10 8 6 4 2

Text copyright © Adrian Mitchell 1999
Illustrations copyright © Stephen Lambert 1999

Designed by Ian Butterworth

The right of Adrian Mitchell to be identified as the author and of Stephen
Lambert as the illustrator of this work has been asserted in accordance with the
Copyright, Designs and Patents Act 1988

Picture Corgi Books are published by Transworld Publishers,
61-63 Uxbridge Road, London W5 5SA,
a division of The Random House Group Ltd,
in Australia by Random House Australia (Pty) Ltd,
20 Alfred Street, Milsons Point, Sydney, NSW 2061,
in New Zealand by Random House New Zealand Ltd,
18 Poland Road, Glenfield, Auckland 10,
and in South Africa by Random House (Pty) Ltd,
Endulini, 5A Jubilee Road, Parktown 2193

Printed in Singpore